Saverio Gaeta

CIVITAVECCHIA

The statue of Our Lady cries tears of blood

Original title in Italian: *CIVITAVECCHIA. Le lacrime di sangue della statuetta di Maria* (St Paul Publisher)

Translated by Seánán Zaltron

© 2023 Lumen Cordium GmbH

Marktgasse, 20

9000 - Sankt Gallen, Switzerland

+41 789246042 (Switzerland)

+39 3355600967 (Italy)

www.lumencordium.com

info@lumencordium.com

ISBN: 978-3-907227-11-4

1. History

Thursday, February 2nd 1995, was the feast of Candlemas, popularly known as this because the rite of blessing candles is celebrated on this day in all churches, recalling the description of Jesus as the "light to reveal God to the nations" (*Luke* 2:32) which Simeon proclaimed during the presentation in the Temple.

A religious service was scheduled in the afternoon in the parish of Sant' Agostino in Borgo Pantano, seven kilometres north of Civitavecchia. Shortly before 4 p.m., all four members of the Gregori family arrived there: 31-year-old Fabio, an electrician at Enel[1], 30-year-old Anna Maria, daughter Jessica, six years old on March 21st and son Davide, three years

---

[1] Enel is the main supplier of electricity in Italy.

old on February 9th (Manuel Maria will join them on December 4th 2002).

"When we found out that the time had been changed *(the Mass had been moved to 4.30 p.m.,* Author's note*)"*, Fabio (the father) later testified, "we stopped for the Rosary, and since Davide was fussing, I thought of taking the children and going home to give them a snack".

In Via Ugo Fontanatetta 10, their home was only a few hundred metres away, and in a few minutes, the father and the two children were ready to return to church. In the diocesan theological commission's documentation, Jessica's account of what happened around 4.20 p.m. is transcribed: 'We had left the house. I went after my father, but while he was putting Davide in the car, I went back and saw that Madonnina (little Madonna) was crying. I called out: "Papa, Papa, the Madonnina is crying blood!". First, she cried with this *(she put her hand over her right eye to indicate which eye the blood came from first)* and then when Papa came, she cried this *(she put her hand over her left eye to tell which eye it was).*

The father's testimony continues: "As I approached her, I saw that the Madonnina had a small rivulet on her face, which was still on the right side. It continued to drip on the left side at the chin level. I saw it when it was under the chin. At first, I was worried and checked if Jessica had any wounds, then I thought of some marks left by the flowers; then I touched it with my finger and felt a shiver and a great flush of fire".

On his return to the church where the Mass was at the consecration, Fabio gave his wife a concise summary of what had happened. At the end of the celebration, he quickly went to the sacristy to meet Fr. Pablo Martin Sanguiao, who had been the parish priest at Sant' Agostino's for a year. In the letter he wrote on the morning of February 4th, two days later, he described the moment as follows to the diocesan Bishop Girolamo Grillo: 'He asked me to go to his house "because an image of Our Lady was weeping blood". His emotion was due not only to the impression that the unexpected sight of such an event can cause in the soul, but also to the fear that it might be a sign of something fearful looming. He also feared that he had committed some kind of sin, having touched "the blood" flowing down the statue's cheek with his finger.'

Fr. Pablo immediately reached the cottage and approached the Madonnina in the garden in front of the house. He knew the statue well, as he had bought it on a pilgrimage to Medjugorje in September 1994 to give it to the Gregori family. It was 43 cm high, with a 9.5 cm wide base and weighed about two and a half kilos. It reproduced the white statue of the Queen of Peace, which is located in front of the parish of St James on Podbrodo hill, where the first apparitions took place. Jessica had dropped it when once trying to caress it and caused the veil to chip and cracked along the dress; after that, Fabio decided to cement it inside a grotto made of sea pebbles.

This is the priest's testimony: "I immediately saw two streams of a dark red colour, which starting from the eyes flowed down the face, one to the hem of the garment under the neck and the other even lower down to the level of the heart.

At first, as they flowed from the eyes, they looked quite watery, although they were very well defined because at the extreme edges, what would be blood appeared as a very sharp line, not much bigger than a hair. As they descended, following the natural path of the face (i.e. not vertically), they became two dark red streaks, occasionally forming the swelling of a drop; all in proportion to the statue's size, i.e. a rivulet one millimetre thick. There were a few specks of 'blood' in the hollow of the eyes. Still, the most surprising thing is that looking at the image from the bottom up (to do this, you have to be almost face down on the ground), you can see that the inside of the upper eyelid is full of this 'blood', as if it were flowing from there.

Around 6.45 p.m. on February 3rd, Fr. Pablo was at the Gregori's house at the moment of the second tear. He recounted the following on October 7th before the Diocesan Theological Commission: "I returned from church with Fabio after preparing a carnival party for the children. Fabio got out of the car before me; then, I passed in front of the

Madonnina before entering the house, and I stopped to say a Hail Mary and see how it was. There was nothing new. I went into the house and after two or three minutes Fabio, who was outside collecting wood for the fireplace, hurriedly called his wife and me because Madonnina was crying again. I remember that we all went out in a great hurry: the statue's niche was illuminated by the electric bulbs it was equipped with (just as I had seen it a few minutes earlier). Then I saw the difference from what I had seen a few minutes before. I saw a spot of blood on the right cheek, which looked like a bruise; at the bottom, it looked like this blood was beginning to form a few drops. The whole thing was tiny in proportion to the statue's size. The two rivulets of blood already there from the first lacrimation seemed to me to have become bright red, whereas before I had seen them brown, like coagulated blood".

The diocesan enquiry records the names of some of the witnesses who recorded their direct experience: ten are mentioned in this second event. About three hours later, at about 9.15 p.m., there was the third tear in the presence of Fabio (who did not witness the further circumstances from this point on) and two others. Then, in the following three days, a sequence of ten other episodes, which also took place during the night prayer vigils: on February 4th at 7.30 p.m. (five witnesses) and 11.30 p.m. (five); on February 5th at 1.15 a.m. (three), 2.30 a.m. (two), 8.45 a.m. (five), 9.45 a.m. (three), 12.30 p.m. (two), 2.40 p.m. (one) and 8.40 p.m. (four); on February 6th at 4.50 a.m. (four). However, many other people attended these tears, including a Member of Parliament, a photojournalist and two journalists, as well as several public officials: the commander of the Civitavecchia Municipal Police, Giancarlo Mori, a Carabiniere (Italian paramilitary police), a non-commissioned Army officer, two correctional officers and four police officers.

In the meantime, Monsignor Grillo documents his absolute disbelief at what he had been told in his journal on February 5th: "What a bad story about crying Madonnas. There is always some joker who takes the liberty of defacing sacred objects.

Poor us, where have we ended up! With the parish priest who also goes after this nonsense". The Bishop's reference was to reports of alleged lacrimations in various parts of Italy, among which those in Assemini (Cagliari), which began on May 22nd 1994, and Subiaco (Rome), reported on January 24th 1995, with a subsequent appendix of numerous reports of weeping images in March alone, had had particular echo: on the 6th in Salerno, on the 12th in Castrovillari (Cosenza), on the 13th in Seriate (Bergamo), on the 14th in Lazise (Verona), on the 20th in Marmore (Terni), on the 22nd in Taranta Peligna (Chieti) and Tivoli (Rome), on the 25th in Viagrande (Catania).

The Bishop's explicit order was "to not give any weight to these things" and even that "the little statue should be destroyed", so Fr. Pablo found himself between a rock and a hard place at dawn on February 6th.

His detailed report shows the agitation of those moments dated March 4th: "Around 5 a.m. Fabio was sleeping with little Davide in the little girl's room;

Jessica was with her mother because the boy had woken up a little earlier, clutching his mother tightly as if he was afraid. Suddenly Fabio was awakened by a male voice which he heard "with his ears", a voice coming from above, at the same time he saw an intense white light coming through the shutter. He got up suddenly, ran to his wife's room and said to her: "Take Davide because I have to take the Madonnina to church". The voice that woke him up had said: "Take her to church; she wants to go to her Son". Then he woke me up in turn by telephone. I remember him saying: "I can't take it anymore! I'm shaking like a leaf. I have to take her to church". I said to him: "No, it's not possible, because it would be like giving an official evaluation, which the Church has not yet given; therefore, the Bishop doesn't want it. And he said: "Then I'll put it in the garden in the square, in front of the church, because that's where it wants to go and I can't keep it here". "But no, wait till daylight! ". "No, I have to bring it to you, and if the church doesn't want to receive it, then it will stay outside".

At this point I said to him: 'All right, I can't keep her in the church; I'll keep her with me, I'll prepare a room for her and no one will know where she is".

At 5.30 a.m. Fabio arrived in front of Sant' Agostino's, his eyes red with tears, accompanied by two excited policemen; he had brought the statue with him, which he had cautiously detached from the base of the grotto. Fr. Pablo's text continues: "Until 8 a.m., the Madonnina stayed with me. I prayed with her and watched her for a long time. When it was convenient, I called the Bishop to tell him what had happened. He was rightly angry that several priests and nuns had appeared among the people making imprudent statements. He told me that he would prohibit the priests from going there during the day, that he would not receive the family and that I had to return the statue and that they should keep it. So it was done immediately. I called Fabio; he came with his brothers, and I explained the situation. We agreed that it could not remain in the house's garden, the church, or a public place. So I called Enrico *(one of Fabio's three brothers)* and told him to take her into custody for the time being and to hide her in a safe place, so people would not attack her. On a country road, away from prying eyes, we transferred the statue, conveniently packed and protected, from the boot of my car to his. He hid it in a place unknown to everyone, except me, under an oath of secrecy".

The Bishop tried to find out more in the following days, confidentially asking for information from the deputy magistrate of Civitavecchia Aldo Vignati and the Gregori family doctor Umberto Natalini. He received positive news from both of them, and a meeting was arranged. This is the description he gave in his journal: "They are simple people; they appear almost traumatised. They may have been the object of evil or malicious deception, but they may also be telling the truth. [...] I felt sorry for the protagonist of the story. He cried when he was alone with me, believing himself to be a man full of sins and almost the object of a curse from God. I had to wipe away his tears, which seemed sincere to me.

At 8.30 a.m. on February 10th, Fabio handed the statue to the Bishop.

The latter subjected it to a brief exorcism ritual (in the meeting on March 25th, he will also do it on little Jessica), ascertaining the absence of sinister influences. A similar initiative had already been taken on February 5th by Fr. Francesco Tomba, exorcist of the Diocese of Civitavecchia, who in the garden of the Gregori's house had invoked God and St Michael the Archangel to verify 'that those red tears are not the work of the devil nor human wickedness'.

In the afternoon, Monsignor Grillo took the Madonnina to Rome for a joint examination by Professors Angelo Fiori, director of the Institute of Forensic Medicine at the Gemelli Hospital, and Giancarlo Umani Ronchi of the institute at La Sapienza University. Once again, Monsignor Grillo's comment was doubtful: "A first result: there are no devices, that is, the lacrimation is not due to mechanical causes or to the nature of the statue's material either. So I thought there's nothing left to do but blame it all on some joker".

A surprise came the following evening: "At 11 p.m. I received a strange phone call from Cardinal

Angelo Sodano *(then Vatican Secretary of State,* author's note*)*, who invited me not to be too sceptical and open to the possibility of the supernatural. Well, we will see! However, I do not hide that this strange phone call has worried me somewhat. Even in the Vatican, they have nothing else to think about; they even watch TV". The Cardinal made another phone call on the evening of February 23rd "on behalf of the Pope, to thank me for what I had said in an interview, filmed and commented on by the journalist Enzo Biagi in the TV program *"Il fatto"*, about the tears of bloodshed by the Madonna. He had liked a certain openness of mine to the supernatural (I had said that, among the many Madonnas who are crying in Italy, in some cases, there could be something serious). [...] I still think: why did the Pope enter into this question on earth? Is he aware of some secret? Or has the Pope gone mad too?".

After receiving confirmation from the experts that the liquid taken from the Madonnina was blood, Monsignor Grillo met on March 1st with the Congregation for the Doctrine of the Faith with

Cardinal Prefect Joseph Ratzinger. All the elements of the affair were taken into consideration. In the end, he was asked for an accurate overall report: "Later on, they will let me know the further steps to be taken. Wisdom and prudence of the Church, which in these phenomena must never be hasty in its evaluation", was his comment in his journal.

Over the next two weeks, the Bishop had further meetings to discuss developments, particularly with Cardinals Sodano and Andrzej Maria Deskur, president of the Pontifical Academy of the Immaculate Conception and a great friend of St. John Paul II. Meanwhile, the media continued to cover the story. After the TV program *'" Chi l'ha visto"* of March 7th, in which strong doubts were raised about the authenticity of the tears, Monsignor Grillo noted: "I too have played the part of the Church, constantly vigilant and cautious in this matter... I don't know what to say. Indeed my faith does not need these things, even if I have the impression that there may be a bit of the supernatural in this affair. Otherwise, why would the Pope be a believer? ".

But the real twist occurred on March 15th, immediately after the morning Mass that the Bishop had celebrated in the private chapel in the presence of his sister Grazia and his brother-in-law Antonio. This is how Monsignor Grillo reconstructed it: "My sister had repeatedly insisted on praying before the Madonnina.

Almost a little annoyed, I told her these exact words: "All right, let's go and pray; praying doesn't hurt ". I then asked Sr. Teresa if I could go and pray in her room, where the Madonnina was enclosed in the top of a cupboard. Sr. Teresa let us into her room, took a chair and opened the cupboard handing me the Madonnina, which was placed in a special basket of straw to avoid possible scratches or things of the kind. I also did this because the Gregori family had almost threatened me: "Woe betide her if she ruins the statue! ". So I took the basket in my hand, on my right stood Sr. Teresa, on my left my brother-in-law Antonio, whom I had invited at my sister's insistence (he had never yet seen the statue), and next to him my sister. So there were four of us in all.

Remaining in this position, we began to pray silently. I was praying the Salve Regina in Latin with my eyes half-closed (as is my custom). I had arrived at the words: *"Illos tuos misericordes oculos ad nos converte"* (*Turn thine eyes of mercy toward us*) when my brother-in-law gave me a nudge with his elbow and said: "Can't you see what's happening?". "What? ', I said, opening my eyes. I then saw that a tear had sprung from the right eye, which had lingered on the cheek to form a sort of small ruby, which would later pass over the same cheek, forming a very thin trickle of blood and recreating no more and no less, the tear that had been removed at the Gemelli Hospital".

The event shook the Bishop terribly, and he collapsed into an armchair in the next room, where he was shortly taken care of by cardiologist Marco Di Gennaro. Who then also had the opportunity to check for the presence of fresh blood on the statue: "I found Monsignor Grillo very pale and tired, sitting near the table in the hall at the entrance of his residence. He was excited and deep in thought. He still held the Madonnina in his hands and showed it to me. There were two bright red patches on her face, superimposed on the last tears, recognisable by the darker, brownish colour of the clot.

The disclosure of the episode took place only on April 4th (and was confirmed by the Bishop on the evening Tg1 (*Italian TV News broadcast author's note*) on April 5th), after Professor Umani Ronchi had participated in a new investigation ordered on the statue by the judiciary on March 28th and had noticed a more recent trace, which he spoke about in the television program *"Misteri"*. In the book *"Il mistero delle Lacrime" (The mystery of the tears),* the Vaticanist Andrea Tornielli reported the testimony of the forensic doctor: "When we held the statue in our hands to take samples at the radiological laboratory of the Gemelli polyclinic, there were rivulets of blood running down to the lower edge of the jaw on both sides. On that occasion, we removed a certain amount of blood, and after the blood sample was taken, the two rivulets did not reach beyond the middle of the cheek of the Madonnina.

When I went to the Bishop to take the other blood sample requested by the Public Prosecutor's Office, the blood arrived again at the jaw level. And, to tell the truth, a slightly different colouring also differentiated the older blood from what could be presumed to be more recent blood".

In fact, between the 1st and 2nd of March, two complaints were sent to the Civitavecchia Public Prosecutor's Office. The anti-plagiarism hotline pointed out that "it is not possible to prove that no device has been found inside the sculpture because if there has been an exchange of statues, it could have taken place before the removal"; the consumer association Codacons suggested that "some people, as yet unknown, intended to offend the Catholic religion and abuse popular credulity, using trickery and deception to make people believe that the statue of the Madonna cried".

The case would have been within the jurisdiction of the magistrate's court. Still, the public prosecutor's office took over the investigation, suggesting the more severe offences of fraud and criminal conspiracy (although there was only one suspect, Fabio Gregori!). On March 9th, his home, his brothers Enrico, Giovanni and Salvatore, and his mother, Enrica Dell'Anno, were searched with "negative results" (police report, March 10th 1995). On March 29th, the telephones of Fabio, Enrico and father Pablo Martin were tapped, from which "no elements of crime emerged" (Commissariat report, May 9th 1995).

The statue was even confiscated, and on 6th April, it was sealed in a cupboard in the Bishop's residence and taken into judicial custody, even though a solemn procession had already been planned for Good Friday, 14th April, for the transfer of the Madonnina to the Parish of Sant'Agostino. A prayer vigil in reparation for this act was organised in the Cathedral on the evening of April 10th, under the presidency of Cardinal Deskur, who, in the name of St. John Paul II, blessed and gave the Gregori's a statue identical to the original, specially brought from Medjugorje. After the intervention of the Tribunal of Freedom, the release of the statue took place on April 18th.

On June 17th, the Madonnina was permanently placed in a particular niche in Sant Agostino's.

The activities of the investigators continued with the request to proceed forcibly, in the probation incident of July 4th 1995, with the taking of blood samples from the four Gregori brothers, their uncle Pietro and the youngest son of one of the brothers. Fabio's lawyer, Bruno Forestieri, objected to this order. On December 13th 1995, his objections were forwarded by the Judge for Preliminary Investigations to the Constitutional Court, which on July 9th declared the illegitimacy of the Prosecutor's Office's request for a forced blood sample.

From this moment on, there was no further investigative activity. Still, despite an initial request for the case to be archived submitted by the lawyer Forestieri on October 3rd 1997, the proceedings against Fabio Gregori were kept open for no reason until October 16th 2000, when the Judge for Preliminary Investigations finally dismissed the case, accepting the request of the Public Prosecutor Antonio Larosa, who - while acknowledging that 'no unequivocal evidence of responsibility for the suspect has been acquired' - dropped a decidedly inappropriate statement: "One cannot help but conclude that the manifestation of the sanctity of the Virgin is something different from such a blasphemous insult". A sentence that provoked an understandably irritated reaction from Fr. De Fiores: "This dismissal or extrapolation that unduly passes from facts to a religious judgement can only be explained by an obvious prejudice of the Prosecutor. In practice, he considers that tears or similar phenomena are incompatible with the Mother of Jesus (as he declared in a private conversation with the Bishop)".

It is interesting to resume also a consideration of the GIP (*preliminary investigations magistrate*): "For completeness of analysis, it must also be considered that the tears noted by other persons informed on the facts (and among them, the Commander of the Municipal Police of Civitavecchia, agents of the Prison Police and the State Police) must be ascribed either to a fact of collective suggestion *(which, however, medicine and psychology do not consider possible).* On *the* other hand, the hypothesis of false declarations must be realistically excluded, given the difficulty of hypothesising criminal agreements between numerous people, including public officials, who mostly do not know each other. It should be pointed out that any possible judgement on the miraculous nature of what happened can only be the responsibility of the Church, which has the burden of explaining to its community whether or not the phenomenon in question should be qualified as a miracle".

Returning to Monsignor Grillo, the bitterness that permeated his days in that spring of 1995 emerges from a note of April 26th, after the meeting of the Bishops' Conference of Lazio in which he had reported on the lacrimation: "As I predicted, the usual three dominated the situation with a certain anti-Marian bitterness, well disguised by props and trappings of a Protestant nature. The Lord and Our Lady will forgive them. However, I had the impression that almost all the others were on a different line from these three. Only that, as usual, probably due to a lack of courage, they shut themselves up and preferred to remain silent.

Even Cardinal Ruini, who had informed me that he had prepared a good and supportive report, could not defend his point unless he backed down out of opportunism".

In the following days, the Bishop complained about this to Cardinal Sodano and Monsignor Stanislao Dziwisz, the secretary of St. John Paul II. Not even a month later, on May 25th, he found himself face to face with the Pope during the annual meeting of the Italian Bishops' Conference: "When it was my turn, he looked me in the eye and asked me this straightforward question: "Is Our Lady still crying? ". My reply was as follows: "Maybe she's still crying, but I can't talk about it. Otherwise, someone will put me in jail" (to tell the truth, I don't know why I gave this answer because I don't remember seeing Our Lady crying again, so mine was likely just a joke). However, I remember the Pope becoming very serious, apostrophising me as follows: "Ah, you other

Italian bishops are hard-headed; you are always doubtful!".

Two weeks later, on the evening of June 9th (as documented on the page of the Bishop's journal), Monsignor Grillo entered the Vatican with a tennis bag that held the Madonnina crying: "This will be an unforgettable day. I had dinner with the Holy Father, who wanted to know the whole story of the Madonnina. I had the impression that he knew everything, even though he did not want to give too much away. I informed him of my contact with both Cardinal Ratzinger and Cardinal Sodano. He quoted von Balthasar [theologian], who says that Our Lady follows her children closely over time, their worries, their concerns. Her weeping is nothing other than an invitation to conversion. We recited a Hail Mary to the Queen of Peace at the meal's end. Then he blessed the statue, the golden crown that will adorn her head and the rosary that will hang from her hand.

To document the episode, on October 8th 2000, Monsignor Grillo gave St. John Paul II a letter in which he summarised what had happened five years earlier (by mistake, the date of the meeting indicated here is June 11th), inviting him to "consider the possibility of coming to Civitavecchia also for a very brief visit to the Madonnina". On the following October 20th, the Pope had a copy returned to him, on which he had affixed his seal as a guarantee of authenticity.

The official visit did not take place, but in the Bishop's memoirs, there is a curious episode: "From what I was told by the nuns who in those years were in charge of the small sanctuary of Sant Agostino's, one evening a busload of Swiss guards arrived there, who at first introduced themselves as people who had come to pray to the Madonnina but immediately positioned themselves around the church until a person disguised as a hunter entered to venerate the Madonnina. It was the Pope, as Fr Stanislao himself practically confirmed to me. It seems, moreover, that the Pope has been to Pantano a second time; I also spoke of this to Don Stanislao, who only replied with a smile. I know nothing else, but it is good that the world should know all this".

At the suggestion of the Congregation for the Doctrine of the Faith, Bishop Grillo quickly set up a diocesan theological commission, which met for the first time on April 19th 1995 and worked for a year and a half with thirteen meetings in all. About fifty witnesses and experts were heard, and at the last meeting, on November 22nd 1996, a wide-ranging report was approved, in which "the Commission was in complete agreement on the truthfulness of the event, and the majority of its members also declared themselves in favour of the supernaturalness of the event".

There were six favourable judgements: "It is not a "presumed" tear but an authentic tear" (Fr. Antonio Ascenzi), "The finger of God is here" (Fr. Nicola Cerasa), "My overall conviction is positive, in the face of an extraordinary intervention of God in history" (Fr. Stefano De Fiores), "The event seems to have no scientific explanation" (Fr. Lino Fumagalli), "The event of the lacrimation cannot be explained on a natural level" (Fr. Sandro Santori), "The phenomenon cannot be explained naturally. Therefore it is worthy of faith" (Fr. Flavio Ubodi).

Three opinions were not contrary or suspensive: "I have found nothing contrary to reason or faith" (Fr. Mario Delmirani), "My response is suspensive, unless "better judgement" is required" (Sr. Fernanda Barbiero), "I believe I cannot express a decisive opinion one way or the other" (Fr. Carlo Rocchetta). Finally, there are two doubtful or negative opinions: "There is no clear evidence of supernaturality" (Fr. Jesús Castellano Cervera), "Not only do we not find elements of supernaturality in the event, but we even feel we must decisively exclude them" (Fr. Ernesto Piacentini). In his book *"La vera storia di un doloroso dramma d'amore" (The true story of a painful drama of love)*, Monsignor Grillo attested that in 2005 Fr. Castellano Cervera told him that "by now his doubts had fallen away, stating categorically that the fact was a serious matter".

On June 14th 1997, the Bishop sent all the documentation he had collected to the Congregation for the Doctrine of the Faith, pointing out the reasons that "would induce him to make public a declaration on the authenticity and truthfulness of these phenomena". On the following October 27th, Cardinal Ratzinger replied, informing him that on October 8th, it had instead been decided by the members of the Congregation, and confirmed by St. John Paul II on October 10th, to "set up a new commission whose members will be appointed by Cardinal Camillo Ruini". The result was a peremptory disposition: "This Dicastery, therefore - while awaiting the creation of this new Commission, which will carry out its task bearing in mind some important observations that emerged in the course of the meeting mentioned above of the most eminent fathers - exhorts your Excellency to refrain from any public declaration based on which the faithful may deduce that the facts concerning the so-called "Madonnina of Civitavecchia" have obtained official recognition by ecclesiastical authority".

There has never been any news of the members and the work of this Commission, so much so that on February 2nd 2000, Monsignor Grillo sent a letter to St. John Paul II in which he stated that "one of the reasons for my distress is the silence of the Commission that the Holy Father has prudently established. I must confess that neither my family nor I have been questioned about the tearing which took place in our presence and which we cannot in conscience deny. Moreover, at the beginning of the last year, 1999, the Congregation for the Doctrine of the Faith, taking a prematurely negative and unprecedented line in the recent history of Marian apparitions, asked me to hand over the statue of the Madonnina to be kept in a safe place removed from worship. Only the intervention of His Holiness, to whom I am immensely grateful, blocked this request, which would have had serious legal (the Madonnina belongs neither to me nor to the diocese but the Gregori family, the legitimate owner) and pastoral consequences. Since then, there has been absolute silence on the part of the Commission. I hope its members will find the time for a serious study of the phenomenon. Above all, I expect them not to proceed with coercive measures to the detriment of the faithful but at least to recognise freedom of worship towards the Madonnina in the wake of what happened at the Tre Fontane. Anything positive from the Commission will contribute to the good of the pilgrims and the diocese".

A year later, on February 28th 2001, a new heartfelt note was sent by the Bishop to St. John Paul II: "A most excellent member of the Lazio Episcopal Conference has informed me that the Congregation for the Doctrine of the Faith is about to close the question of the lacrimation of blood from the "Little Madonna of Civitavecchia" with the declaration: *"Non constat de supernaturalitate" (that is, the wait-and-see verdict of "there is no evidence of supernaturalness",* author's note*)*. Such a declaration would cause considerable damage to the great devotion already established by the faithful worldwide, to the great scandal of souls and serious damage to the Church. It would give the great press, all the mass media and especially the anti-clericals, even at an international level, the opportunity to cast doubt on the word of the Bishop of Civitavecchia and to ridicule him, since he has always said (and will repeat it until his death) that the Madonna has truly wept in his hands. Apart from the fact that such a statement would force the faithful, should the Bishop be forced to remove the Madonnina from common devotion, to go, instead of to the church, where the Madonnina is currently located, to the place in the grotto (private garden) where the Madonnina wept, without the control of the ecclesiastical authority? [...] It seems rather strange to me and my impression that someone, perhaps, had already decided on the matter before examining it".

On February 17th 2005, Cardinal Tarcisio Bertone, speaking on the television program *"Porta a Porta"*, confirmed that in 2000 the Congregation, of which he was a secretary, had made the judgement but that it had never been made public. The authoritative Vaticanist Orazio Petrosillo said: "It is said in the Vatican that 'very high up' did not want it. According to some, the Pope himself did not approve of the publication.

A few weeks later, Cardinal Joseph Ratzinger, who as Prefect of the Doctrine of the Faith had endorsed the statement, was elected Pope Benedict XVI and astonished Monsignor Grillo when greeting him on May 30th 2005, at the end of the general assembly of the Italian bishops, he looked him in the eye. He said in a clear voice: "Our Lady of Civitavecchia will do great things".

Meanwhile, on March 15th, the Bishop declared the parish of Sant'Agostino a Marian shrine, officially allowing public worship of the Madonnina. On December 8th of the same year, as documented by Anna Maria Turi in her book *Miracoli e segreti della Madonnina di Civitavecchia (Miracles and Secrets of the Madonnina of Civitavecchia)*, Monsignor Grillo sent a letter to Fabio Gregori in which he revoked the order issued on April 6th 1996 "in the point in which it says that both celebrations of Masses and acts of public worship, recitation of the Rosary and other forms of ritual prayer are forbidden in your house and your garden". On April 26th 2014, during a solemn concelebration, the new Bishop of Civitavecchia,

Luigi Marrucci, publicly crowned the Madonnina, repeating the gesture made privately by St. John Paul II in 1995.

2. Prophecy and science

On March 13th 1995, Monsignor Grillo received a telephone call from the well-known exorcist Fr Gabriele Amorth. In his journal, he summarised his words as follows: "He begged me not to be very sceptical because he had known since last summer - from a soul, he spiritually directed - that a Madonna would cry in Civitavecchia and that this sign would not be a good omen for Italy; therefore it would be opportune to do penance and pray a lot".

It was not an easy time for the country, which was still in the midst of a political and judicial storm, triggered in 1992 by the so-called "Tangentopoli scandal" the related "Clean Hands" enquiry, shaken by the Mafia's massacre outbreaks, and the attacks on magistrates Giovanni Falcone and Paolo Borsellino. These events led St. John Paul II to promote the "Great Prayer for Italy" throughout 1994, which ended on December 10th in the sanctuary of Loreto. And which somehow inspired Father Pablo Martin to make a striking remark: "The trickle of tears and blood, which formed on the left cheek from the first day, evokes the figure of Italy with remarkable similarity. It is certainly a sign for Italy, and to have taken place in Civitavecchia is, as if it were, "under the Pope's window"".

In his first letter to Bishop Grillo on February 4th, the parish priest of Sant Agostino's described two mysterious forebodings of which he was aware: "In October, Fabio's wife informed me that a large cross of flowers had appeared in the field they owned behind the house. The most extended arm measured more than fifty metres. No one had sown this cross of white flowers. Months later, you can still see the strip left in the middle of the green. In mid-January, for four days at least, a mysterious white dove perched every day at the feet of the Madonnina and then went to perch on the roof of the house. No one knows where it came from or where it went. There are no dovecotes in the area.

In the weeks immediately following the tears, between March and June 1995, Fabio Gregori began to hear a male voice that gave him some messages, starting with a warning of what would happen: "The road will be long, tortuous, painful, but then the light of the Lord will shine" *(March 15th)*. And when his relationship with the investigators became problematic, the same voice encouraged him: "The way of truth is in the Church of God. The truth comes from God. Do not fear man, fear God" *(May 6th)*. For years very little was known of these phrases. Father Flavio Ubodi, who has been in charge of closely following the Gregori family since the time of Monsignor Grillo, has only recently made them public in his book *La Madonna di Civitavecchia. Tears and Messages*.

Five other messages came from the same source, with an initial reminder to attend the sacraments: "You are one of my favourites; I will send you an angel to show you what will happen. Blessed is he who will have kept and preached the prophetic words of the Church of God, our Father, who, through our heavenly Mother, Our Lady, prepares the way for us to intercede with our Father, God. Never forsake the sacraments, confession, prayer, fasting and the Body of Jesus Christ in Holy Mass, for my coming will be very soon" *(May 15th)*.

Then the reference to a dangerous future and the explanation that the blood of Madonna's weeping is that of Jesus: "Humanity is about to enter into a gruesome tragedy. They do not realise that they are about to enter a world war that can be stopped. I am telling you a message that the Holy Father the Pope already knows through another daughter of mine. Stop this war! You have the most powerful weapons: love, prayer, humility, the Rosary, and the conversion of your hearts towards God through our heavenly Mother, who is holding you all in her arms, close to her Immaculate Heart. I beg you, no longer allow me to weep my blood for all the children turning away from her Immaculate Heart to give you the salvation our Father is giving you. Love one another, return to be the true people of God, a people of true humility, love, prayer and living the Church of God, founded by him in the sacraments" *(May 19th)*.

A mysterious announcement concerning the Church followed this: "Remember that the Church is of our Father God, and you are one of the heavenly servants, as are many other priests. Our Father will re-establish His Church here, and all the ends of the earth will see salvation if you place humanity into the hands and the Immaculate Heart of our heavenly Mother.

Let your steps be guided in your steps with the simplicity with which a child places his hands in his father's hands. Walk confidently towards man's ultimate goal, eternal life with God" *(May 24th)*. And the following message was accompanied by a vision: "I saw a ray of ample light descend from the sky and take the form of a human body dressed in white, barefoot, with a long white robe and a luminous crown on his head. He had two brilliant white wings. He called me "son of God", "Now you will see a sign that you will not understand".

As he said these things to me, I saw descending from heaven a crown of twelve angels holding hands, and within it was the cross with Jesus nailed to it. It struck me that the nails in the hands were not in the palms but the wrist. When he reached two metres from the ground, he stopped. The face of the Lord was bleeding. I felt sad and full of suffering. After about two minutes, they disappeared" *(May 30th)*.

The last of these phrases seem to come from God the Father and strongly references the family: "My dear son, having accepted my divine will, Jesus is within you; you have become a living tabernacle. Be still and adore your Lord. Express all the joy of possessing Him, open your heart to Him and speak to Him with great confidence for at least a quarter of an hour a day. My dear son, you do not know that men do not make an effort to nourish themselves with Eucharistic Communion, even though they need it. Your heavenly Mother feeds on this bread, to turn it into milk, to nourish her poor children. Behold, your Mamma has transformed it into the Body and Blood of Jesus, now called the Eucharist. Have compassion on the Immaculate Heart of your most holy Mother, wrapped in the thorns that ungrateful men continually inflict on her, and no one makes acts of reparation to tear them out. When you see her in a few days, she will tell you what you must do for me, for her, for the Kingdom of God. I love you because you are my heavenly son, as are the servants and priests of my Church. Love one another, my children, educate and raise my children and yours. I have chosen you because your family will be born the new way of the new and true family of God. If you do not hear from me anymore, do not fear, for I am not going away, but for the last time, I will give the power to journey with you to your heavenly Mother. Now, when you see her, she will be the one to guide you. Love me and love her, for she will lead my people to salvation towards my Son Jesus. I love you, always be above you, and I will follow your every step" *(June 26th)*.

An important message was the one received by Anna Maria in June: "I heard Our Lady's voice: 'Pray, convert, because I am coming for another year, and if you do not listen to me, then there will be no more time'. Then she explained that there was still one more tear, and then the Rosary would be completed, all fifteen mysteries *(this has not yet taken place,* author's note*).* Then the voice continued: 'Pray, convert, return to me, you are about to enter a nuclear war'".

Since July 1995, Our Lady began to appear to Fabio, while there is no precise public information about the numerous manifestations to Jessica. In all, between 1995 and 1996, there were 93 messages, and the diocesan representative, Father Flavio Ubodi guaranteed that "the events have been narrated to me and the messages delivered as they occurred in writing by Fabio Gregori. It is documented that they are from that precise period". On June 15th 1996, the little girl met Sister Lucia of Fatima in the Carmel of Coimbra and confided: "We spoke about the Third Secret and everything else... and we passed on the message to each other, we passed on what the Madonnina wanted". Father Ubodi added that Jessica "specifies that she is still the sole custodian - verbatim - of "one last message concerning the Third Secret of

Fatima, which, out of obedience to the Virgin", she will have to reveal directly and only "to the Pope, when the time comes". According to her father, Our Lady told Jessica: 'I have chosen Fatima for the beginning of the twentieth century, Civitavecchia for its end'.

Monsignor Grillo revealed that the little girl, with an image similar to the one in the third part of the Secret of Fatima (which at that time was still unknown, having only been made public in 2000), spoke to him of "a road in front of which was the Holy Father with a cross in his hand and behind him many bishops, priests, friars, men and women of all ages, and many angels carrying away many children, while the heavenly Mother wept, asking them to pray a lot, to ask forgiveness of her Son to obtain salvation from an immense fire that was hanging over them. Only in this way," Our Lady would add, "can purification be obtained, and she would be able to stop the hand of her Son".

At 6.30 p.m. on July 2nd, during Mass in the parish, Fabio saw the Virgin for the first time, described as a girl of about 16 years, with wavy brown hair, partly covered by a sky-blue veil which falls over her long white tunic, with her feet surrounded by the cloud on which she is standing and in her left hand the Rosary: "She was standing above Father Pablo, with her feet immersed in a white cloud, with her arms open and her hands turned towards the ground... She looked like Our Lady of Fatima... After the Eucharist, she disappeared".

Her first message came two weeks later, while the man was in Abruzzo, at the foot of the Gran Sasso: "Son, it is I, your heavenly Mother, do not be afraid! My dear son, look at these mountains, these forests, this clear and pure water, the sign of life. This is the Kingdom of God. A Kingdom of peace, love and divine purity. A purity that within your hearts, there can be nothing but love. I am your heavenly Mother; I will educate your family because our Father, God, will re-found through you, sweet children, God's new and true family. From you, dear children, must begin a journey of evangelisation of the Word of God our Father, not only in prayer but also in the greatest union of love in the family, educating yourselves and yours and our children. The path will not be easy because Satan wants to destroy families, but you have a divine weapon that God has granted you. Satan presented himself to you, as he presented himself to me, in the form of a serpent, and with the divine grace granted to you, you killed him, as I killed him, keeping him subdued under your feet. So you need not fear, for we are all close to you. How could I, your heavenly Mother, permit you to be harmed? But you pray and continue to grow spiritually, for when my fruit is ripe, God our Father will show you who your family is. I love you; I hold you all close to my Immaculate Heart, be sweet, pure and simple, like a newborn child. Continue to be like this, because in this way you make me happy and smile with joy" *(July 16th)*.

Then there were words in powerful tones: "Dear child, I am giving you sad news. Satan is taking over all of humanity, and now he is trying to destroy the

Church of God through many priests. Do not allow this! Help the Holy Father! Satan knows that his time is coming to an end because my Son Jesus is about to intervene. Please help me, do not let my Son Jesus intervene, because I, your Mother, want to save so many souls and take them to my Son and not leave them to Satan. Pray that God our Father may grant me some more time because this is the last period God granted me. My mantle is now open to all of you, completely full of graces, to place you all close to my Immaculate Heart. [It is] about to close, then my Son Jesus will unleash His divine justice. There is a danger hanging over the Holy Father, my son, a fierce attack by Satan, for he, my true and holy son, is opening the doors of the hearts of the true Church of God, and Satan does not want it. You, my son, must help him. Pray together with the Holy Father on October 7th *(on that Saturday afternoon, St. John Paul II prayed the Rosary in New York Cathedral together with families from the 400 parishes of the diocese,* ed*)*. Do not be afraid if they laugh at you, but remember that in the eyes of God, our Father, you are a beloved son, full of love and grace bestowed upon you. Remember that you are sanctified, having accepted the divine will with true love; you are a scented rose full of petals of fragrant graces. I love you, love everyone, for every act of love, is a soul you are saving from Satan and bringing to God yours and our Father. I love you!" *(July 30th)*.

As a weapon to defeat Satan, the Rosary was reiterated immediately afterwards: "My dear beloved children, I am apprehensive. We have chosen you for a journey of evangelisation, to help me bring my lost children to Jesus and make you grow united in love and family. You are getting too tired; God does not want this. God wants serenity and happiness. You lose your strength for prayer by getting excessively tired so Satan can attack you. Do not worry if my children do not believe your words; just pray because only by praying can you help them love Jesus. I teach you to pray, my sweet children. Seek me every moment during the day, working, thinking of the children, and thank Jesus because these are prayers of love.

Everything done with God's love and seeking His will becomes a living prayer. Pray the Holy Rosary, divine weapon to defeat Satan, go to confession at least once a week, take part in the Eucharist if possible" *(August 16th)*.

At the end of August, an apparition brought Fabio and Jessica together: "Dear children, I love you; my love is a divine love full of the Lord's light. The Lord has clothed me with His light and the Holy Spirit with His power. My task is to take all my children away from Satan and bring them back to the perfect glorification of the Most Holy Trinity. My will is that you all consecrate yourselves to my Immaculate Heart so that I can lead you all to Jesus, cultivating you in my heavenly garden. I present myself to you as Our Lady of the Roses of the Immaculate Heart, Queen of Heaven, Mother of Families, Bearer of Peace in your hearts. Convert, my sweet children, for time is running out. Help me, be humble of heart, charitable, return to be the true people of God with one heart, which pulses rays of the Lord's light to spread them throughout the world, to help me destroy the darkness. Pray with love" *(August 25th)*.

The next day Our Lady seemed very worried: "My dear children, I weep because I am speaking to you in every part of the world, giving you extraordinary signs, but you do not listen to me. I am presenting myself to you in every form, but you do not accept me with true love in your hearts. You see my tears as a sign of curiosity, but your hearts remain hard, and you do not allow the light of the Lord to enter. My sweet, beloved children, consecrate yourselves to my Immaculate Heart, which is full of divine love. Jesus jealously guards you in His divine plan full of love. Continue to be simple and full of love for everyone. Pray, pray, pray. Please accept this heartfelt invitation of mine, which I am still giving you today from this holy place that God has consecrated, and addressed to all the nations of the world. With the same love and in the same way, you embrace your child and open your hearts and arms so that you may be ready to embrace Christ in the splendour of his glory because His great coming is about to arrive.

Pray and never tire of praying. My sweet children, love one another because love in Christ my Son is your key to enter into that small door which leads to the Kingdom of God" *(August 26th)*.

In a later message, the Virgin referred to Fatima and the Italian situation: "My children, the darkness of Satan is now obscuring the whole world and obscuring the Church of God. Prepare yourselves to live what I revealed to my little daughters of Fatima. Dear children, after the painful years of Satan's darkness, now the years of the triumph of my Immaculate Heart are imminent. Your nation is in great danger. In Rome, darkness is falling more and more on the Rock, which my Son Jesus left you to build, educate and spiritually grow His children. Bishops, your task is to continue the growth of God's Church since you are God's heirs. Return to be one heart full of true faith and humility with my son St. John Paul II, the greatest gift that my Immaculate Heart has obtained from the Heart of Jesus. Consecrate all of you to me, to my Immaculate Heart, and I will protect your nation under my mantle now full of graces. Listen to me, I beg you, and I implore you! I am your heavenly Mother; I beg you, do not make me cry anymore when I see so many of my children dying because of your faults for not accepting me and allowing Satan to act. I love you, help me, we need everyone one of you, sweet children" *(September 19th)*.

The meaning of suffering was at the centre of a further apparition: "My beloved children, I love you, and I suffer in seeing you suffering. My Immaculate Heart will transform your sufferings that you accept with true love into immense joy because these are trials that the Lord Jesus permits. Your spiritual growth is the light of the Lord. I look after you, leading you by the hand like children because this is how you are and must remain. I can spread the light of faith through you in these days of great apostasy. You are the light of the Lord because you are children consecrated totally to me. Let me guide you with much love, a true love you have for Jesus in the Eucharist.

I rejoice with happiness because you are simple and humble and let yourselves be guided like a blade of grass moved by the wind. I, your heavenly Mother, Our Lady of Roses, Queen of Heaven, Mother of Families, Bearer of Peace into your hearts, through you I can accomplish the great divine plan of the great triumph of my Immaculate Heart if you listen to me with true love, and grant my requests by walking on the path that I trace in your minds and hearts, I love you all. Love everyone. Always forgive everyone, as Jesus always did, even when they crucified Him" *(September 8th)*.

Then Our Lady re-iterated the invitation to consecrate oneself to her Immaculate Heart: "My dear children, I love you all; you are so sweet. If only you could understand in your hearts how great is the love we all have for you, you would not be able to contain your happiness. I am your heavenly Mother, and I have presented myself to you, in this lovely city, as Our Lady of the Roses of the Immaculate Heart. God, our Father, has placed me with His glory and His divine love as the Queen full of graces for every one of you. He created all things through His Divine Mercy because of His infinite love. When He saw that His children had fallen into sin, He made Himself through the workings of the Holy Spirit a child from me, and I gave birth to Jesus, my only Son, begotten in the flesh by God.

His death saved all things on the cross, a death of infinite love and mercy which He has for all His children. My sweet children, I am happy to see small prayer groups growing in this city and many conversions. Still, I need many prayers for the children who are overshadowed by darkness so that many souls may return to Jesus to overcome evil and make my Immaculate Heart triumph. This is my task, granted to me by God our Father: to save everyone and bring them to Jesus. I beg you to listen to me. Go to the bishop and tell him: "Gather your priests and ask them to consecrate, for the love of God, their parish and families to my Immaculate Heart; and you, as an apostle of God, raise all the consecrations into one consecration of the whole city to my Immaculate Heart so that we may walk together having completed the consecration which you have already received through Jesus in Baptism. So that this city may become a valley of grace for the whole world, to defeat Satan." *(December 7th)*.

In the spring of 1996, the last apparition with a public message: "My task is finished, adore God and thank Him for this grace which He has given you, to you and all humanity. And for the immense love, He has for all His children and His Church. In union with the Son and the Holy Spirit, He has sent me, your Mother, Our Lady of the Roses, to call you back with love and bring you back onto His path. Love each other and be peacemakers; grow in faith. I am going away, but my Son and your brother Jesus will always remain with you in all the tabernacles of the Church and will always live within you if you wish. He will nourish and guide you through the Holy Spirit, leading all His Church to sanctification until you reach His Kingdom and your Kingdom" *(May 17th 1996)*.

In short, according to Fabio Gregori, "Our Lady has addressed herself from here to the whole of humanity, to the Church and to that portion of the Church which is the family, placing this intervention of hers in the wake of the Fatima message. She warned us that Satan is powerful and wants to unleash hatred, therefore, war to destroy humanity. And to achieve this, he wants to tear down the Church of God, starting with the small domestic Church that is the family, which is the cradle of society, and, modelled on the Family of Nazareth, the foundation of the Christian community. The threat is a nuclear conflict between the West and the East, the Third World War. And Our Lady added that the devil would do everything to undermine the unity of the Christian family founded on marriage. And that, without a new conversion, many priests would betray their vocation, even with grave scandal, and that the Church would experience a great new apostasy, that is, the denial of the fundamental Christian truths reaffirmed over the centuries in tradition and doctrine".

In the report sent to Bishop Grillo on March 4th 1995, Fr. Pablo offered some interesting observations on the dynamics of the first tear, which are also helpful in understanding the scientific question: "The initial trickle, on the left cheek, appeared to deviate in contrast with the law of gravity considerably; it did not descend vertically. In a living person, this trace would have meant that the trickle on the right cheek and the one on the left and occurring at different moments would have found the head displaced, i.e. in a different position. This made me think that, if it had been the work of an artist, he could have absent-mindedly contravened the law of gravity in favour of art; if, on the other hand, it had been the work of a forger, using an eyedropper, it would have been impossible, first of all, because the statuette was solidly cemented and could not have been placed at an angle to make the liquid flow in that way, and then, if it had been lifted (and then cemented again in great haste), the path of the "blood" in one cheek would have been, even in this case, the same path on the other. This lack of logic, which a forger would not have done, led me to think that no one could have done it. Moreover, to the eye, there was no ink, paint or anything else; the appearance was that which we all know of freshly coagulated blood, and at the top, it was even seen as 'diluted' in water.

On February 5th, doctors Umberto Natalini, technical consultant to the Court of Civitavecchia, and Graziano Marsili, an analyst at the Europa Diagnostic Centre, carried out the first analysis of the red trickle by using the laboratory test for occult blood in organic materials: "A small amount of dried liquid was taken with a swab which when it came into contact with the reagents, it took on intense blue-greyish colour, typical of a robust positive test. A second test carried out as a counter test, without the presence of the red liquid, gave an entirely negative result. The test answered as if haemoglobin was present.

On the afternoon of February 10th, director Angelo Fiori and his counterpart from La Sapienza University, Giancarlo Umani Ronchi, examined the face and neck of the statue in the Institute of Forensic Medicine at the Gemelli Hospital and accurately described the reddish traces: "In correspondence with the right orbit, at the level of the eyelid commissure a dry stream of material of a haematic appearance begins, which occupies the lower eyelid and the cheekbone up to the nasolabial groove and continues more subtly along the paramedian line reaching the upper edge of the centrally decorated robe and bordered on the outside by the mantle. In correspondence with the left orbit, another stream of haematic aspect, also dry, starts from the medial side of the lower eyelid and turns towards the left cheekbone descending then onto the outer part of the cheek to the lateral part of the neck, which is passed to reach the upper-left edge of the garment at the level of the medial edge of the left part of the mantle".

Two samples were taken by placing a piece of filter paper soaked in a little distilled water on the lower end of both streams and analysed using two methods. The Kastle-Meyer reaction with phenolphthalein and silica gel chromatography: 'It was established that the traces on the face and neck were blood'.

Then, using the technique of microprecipitation on agar slides, the species to which this blood belonged was verified: "Only the anti-human antisera provided visible precipitation lines: the conclusion is that it is human blood". Finally, it was determined using the polymerase chain reaction genetic technique that both the Y and X chromosomes were present in the white blood cells contained in the blood trace, 'allowing us to state that the human blood belongs to a man.

On February 24th, Professor Maurizio Vincenzoni carried out an X-ray examination of the statue at the Institute of Radiology of the Gemelli Hospital 'to establish whether there were any anomalous structures or equipment inside: the result was completely negative'. The examination was repeated on April 3rd using a CT scan with 43 scans, which confirmed that "the statue was solid at all levels, with no central cavity and when analysed in various sections, it showed some irrelevant bubbles due to the methods used in its preparation".

Thanks also to the chipping on the statue, as guaranteed by the director of the Civitavecchia police station Luigi Di Maio, "we have established with absolute certainty that there have been no substitutions and that the statuette that cried in the Pantano garden is precisely the one that Professors Fiori and Umani Ronchi tested".

On March 29th, on the judiciary's orders, the laboratory of the scientific police in Rome. Dr Aldo Spinella, head of the Criminal Police's Biological Investigations section, was assisted by Fiori and Umani Ronchi in detecting DNA polymorphisms in the blood taken from the Madonnina: five were caught (HLA DQα 3.4; HUMvWA 150-154; HUMTH01 170-173; HUMF13A1 192-192; HUMMBP 134-142/232-232). From this analysis, many people still have doubts about Fabio Gregori and the authenticity of the lacrimation, motivated by the man's alleged refusal to submit to a blood test to determine whether the blood found on the statue was not his own.

Therefore, it is helpful to clarify that the males of the Gregori family had naively and spontaneously agreed to the blood sample. After consulting geneticists, Mr Forestieri, a lawyer, explained things to everyone, summarising the problem schematically:

1. Given the minimal quantity of blood traces present on the face of the statue, it was certainly not possible to carry out a thorough analysis.

2. It is impossible, precisely because of the above, to compare the results of the analysis of the blood liquid of the statue and that of other subjects.

3. To make a comparison, in any case, one would have to carry out further control tests, which are now impossible, given the inexistence, in fact, of further blood findings on the face of the statue.

4. Any comparison's real and true result would be so unreliable that it could allow manipulation, with aberrant consequences, given the problematic and not objective judgment'.

Basically, at a time when DNA research was still in its infancy, and there was not even a complete mapping of it (it was not until 2003 that US scientists identified all the polymorphisms), the isolation of just five polymorphisms made the blood trace compatible with 95 per cent of the world's population. To understand the delicacy of the matter, this comment by Mr Forestieri is sufficient: 'If blood had been taken from all the citizens of Civitavecchia and the results compared with those of the Madonnina's blood, they would all have been considered compatible! And could an ordinary citizen make a distinction between the words compatibility and identity? ".

The second statue, donated by Cardinal Deskur, has also inexplicably begun to secrete drops of a viscous substance since September 7th 1995: first on the occasion of major feasts and Marian solemnities, then with increasing frequency, especially when devotees gather for prayer. Professor Fiori carried out an analysis and, in his report of July 4th 2002, concluded that 'it is a liquid containing aromatic substances such as terpenes and sesquiterpenes of probable vegetable origin'.

In the days immediately preceding the death of St. John Paul II on the evening of April 2nd 2005, ordinary, saline tears flowed from the eyes of this Madonna. The same phenomenon occurred the following year, between 28th and 31st March. Father Ubodi clarified that "Jessica maintains that the event is not linked to the death of the Pope, but other things.

Our Lady weeps for grave things, and perhaps also for how the ecclesiastical hierarchy is behaving about the events in Civitavecchia".

3. The message

On the day of the first lacrimation in Civitavecchia, the liturgy commemorated the Presentation of the Lord in the Temple, with the Gospel recalling Simeon's foretelling of the pain of Christ's passion to Mary: "And a sword will pierce your soul too" (*Luke* 2:35). On this occasion, what St. John Paul II called "a second announcement to Mary occurred since it indicates to her the concrete historical dimension in which the Son will fulfil his mission, in incomprehension and pain. If such an announcement, on the one hand, confirms her faith in fulfilling the divine promises of salvation. On the other hand, it also reveals that she will have to live her obedience of faith in suffering alongside the suffering Saviour and that her motherhood will be obscure and painful" (*Redemptoris Mater*).

And it is interesting to note that the Apostolic Exhortation *Marialis Cultus,* signed by St.Paul VI on

February 2nd 1974, stresses that this feast "must be dwelt upon to fully grasp the depth of its content as a joint memorial of the Son and the Mother. The celebration of a mystery of salvation brought about by Christ, to which the Virgin was intimately united as Mother of the suffering Servant of Yahweh. As executor of a mission entrusted to ancient Israel and a model for the new people of God, she was constantly tested in faith and hope by suffering and persecution".

This date is also connected with an impressive dream that Anna Maria Gregori had on the night of January 16th 1995, described by Fr. Pablo Martin to the Diocesan Commission as follows: "Previously she had dreamt of Our Lady holding Jesus in her arms and showing him to her. At that moment she didn't pay much attention, but two days later she came to tell me about another "very vivid" dream she had had. She dreamt that she was in a church where she saw a portrait of Jesus, which was slowly, slowly coming to life. Jesus came out of the picture and took her under his arm. Anna Maria cried out, calling the parish priest joyfully, and said: "Fr. Pablo, Jesus! Jesus has come!" And I would have answered her in her dream: "No, Anna Maria, not now, the time has not come". Then Fabio, her husband, arrived with a baby in his arms, and Jesus said to him: 'I will take her away from you; you will not weep for my mercy, but her death on Candlemas Day'".

The testimony continues: "This was the dream, which has remained engraved in her memory. At first, she interpreted it as meaning that she had to die on Candlemas and said: "All right, Jesus, as you wish, but have mercy; you see that I have these two babies...". She thought that the words "I will take her away from you" referred to herself, that is, that she should die on February 2nd. I told her: "Don't worry, we'll talk about it on the fifth...". Only later did she understand that the words "to her" referred to the Madonnina, to her statue, as happened on February 6th, with great pain and tears from Fabio, as he had to part with it. The dream spoke concretely of "Candlemas Day", as the day "of her death". Of whom? Of Mary!

In fact, on that day, death began for her with those words of Simeon that pierced her Heart".

Pantano is an important place in the Christian tradition. According to scholars, it was on a nearby beach - as recalled by the sign "Bagni di sant'Agostino" (Saint Augustine's baths) at the fork in the Via Aurelia - that the saint from Hippo had an extraordinary encounter, recounted in the writings of ancient authors as far back as the 13th century. In the summer of 387, Augustine, baptised in Milan, had moved to Ostia with his mother Monica, waiting to embark on a ship bound for Africa. The death of his mother on August 27th of that year prompted him to stop and visit some Christian communities in the area around Civitavecchia, staying in the hermitage of the Holy Trinity of Centumcellis, near Allumiere.

One day he decided to take a walk along the seashore, meditating on the mystery of the Holy Trinity, to which he was dedicating his book *De Trinitate*. Suddenly he saw a child playing with the water from the sea, taking it in the hollow of his hand and pouring it into a hole dug in the sand.

Augustine asked him why, and the little one replied that he wanted to put the whole sea into that tiny hole. But when he pointed out that such an undertaking was impossible, the child replied: "It is easier to pour all the sea's water into this small pit than to put the mystery of the Holy Trinity into your mind". Then he disappeared, showing himself to be an angelic creature.

On June 17th 1995, the church of Sant'Agostino, so-called to commemorate this event, was stormed by the media and countless faithful for the celebration, during which the Madonnina was permanently placed inside the church. In his homily, Bishop Girolamo Grillo offered a detailed explanation of the relationship between Our Lady and Christ: "Mary was always present during the most important and dramatic hours of her Son's life. She was especially present at the foot of the cross. This is just a brief side note to help us better understand what abyss of truth this fact conceals. At that moment, it was impossible for the Virgin not to know everything about her Son.

At that moment, she gave the full measure of her faith. Our Lady's faith reaches its peak at that very moment, and it is then that another great mystery occurs: since the Son is about to die, the Virgin's mission as Mother of Jesus on earth also ends. But, at that very moment, another kind of work began for her: the Son invited her to collaborate with him in the world's redemption, entrusting all men to her and making her our mother, the Mother of the Church. The kind of work that her Son was doing for the world's redemption allowed her to collaborate fully for the first time. Mary experienced the depths of her suffering, which was redemptive suffering. And since it is certain that she, at this point, knew her Son's mission perfectly, it is easy to understand the unique place she occupies in the redemption of souls: she entered into it with full clarity of faith, through suffering that is the climax of a mother's suffering".

I would like Civitavecchia to be the starting point for an incredible drive to intensify devotion to Our Lady in preparation for the third millennium, which, as has been rightly stated, will either be Christian or will not be.

Let us dry Our Lady's tears, the tears she sheds for the *misterium iniquitatis (the mystery of iniquity,* author's note*),* which unfortunately reigns in the world and which has its harmful influences on the life of the Church and civil society, in the family, in schools and institutions. A splendid shrine will be built here, but it will be a shrine of people who wish to retrace the path of the Gospel rather than a shrine of bricks. Here we want charity for the poor, and from here, we must commit ourselves to pray for world peace. Here will begin an authentic, extended,-lasting and proper Marian catechesis, involving priests and faithful in a fierce and constant commitment to grow in faith, prayer, contemplation, Eucharistic adoration, conversion and frequent reconciliation with God with our brothers in the sacrament of confession".

In Riccardo Caniato's book *"La Madonna si fa la strada",* Cardinal Deskur makes an interesting insight into the reasons why the Madonna wept tears of blood: "To show how deeply her pain struck her

Heart, wounded by the sword, as predicted by the prophet Simeon at the moment of Jesus' offering in the temple. And the tangibility of this sign wants us to perceive how deeply Our Lady's Heart is hurt by our conduct which is not very Christian, our infidelity and our repeated offences against Christ. Let us take to heart this event, this blood of Our Lady; let us strive to understand her maternal Heart and console it as much as we can with our lives of reparation, fidelity and filial love. Moreover, Our Lady weeps because her Son shed his blood, and she shares in his passion. Our Lady shared in the pain of the Father for having sacrificed his only Son, but at the same time, as Mother, she suffers the same pain of having sacrificed her only Son.

And, in this mystery of communion, we learn and understand that the blood of Jesus corresponds to the blood of Mary".

In 1996, Monsignor Grillo asked the members of the Gregori family to transcribe and interpret according to their conscience the content of the messages of the Madonnina after re-reading and meditating on them carefully. Here is the synthesis proposed, in simple but effectively clear language, starting from the Virgin's request "for the consecration to her Immaculate Heart: personal; of the diocese of Civitavecchia and Tarquinia, by the Bishop; of the world, by Holy Mother Church" and two warnings: "The Church has entered the period of the great trial" and "humanity is about to enter situations of danger, of imminent tragedies, world and nuclear wars, if they do not return to being God's people, a true people of peace and true love".

So, a sequence of recollections:

- "To the virginity of Mary Most Holy. Our Lady emphasises that "Jesus is the only son conceived in my flesh";

- to receive Jesus in the Eucharist daily with the recommendation, when this is not possible, to receive Him spiritually.

Our Lady says: "Men do not have the strength to nourish themselves with Eucharistic communion, yet they need it because it is the only Bread of Eternal Life";

- to expose Jesus in the Eucharist in all churches and to pause in adoration to draw all graces from the source of life and so that he may live amid his brothers and sisters;

- to the unity and defence of the family because Satan wants to destroy it because it becomes a small domestic Church in the sacrament. In so doing, he sows darnel, creating a society that is ever more immoral, dark and cold; creating especially in young people an imbalance in human and spiritual growth;

- to the defence of life because it is a gift from God. On February 6th 1995, which coincided with the Day of Life, the Madonnina wept seven times;

- the existence and presence of angels and their mission. Both priests and laypeople are compared to angels, defined as 'heavenly servants' and 'earthly angels';

- to the Pope's ministry. Its strength confirms that the absolute Gospel Truth is only in the Church of Jesus, entrusted to the Pope and all the bishops united to him in obedience;

- to prayer, especially the Holy Rosary: it is the only weapon for defeating Satan and not falling into sin. Our Lady reminds us that "the actions of the day, carried out with God's love and illuminated by His will, become living prayers";

- to be like children and to love children especially, with the same care as Jesus, since they are a gift from God entrusted to us;

- to the reading of Sacred Scripture and to walk only in the sure path of the teaching and magisterium of Holy Mother Church;

- never to abandon the sacraments, with a particular emphasis on confession;

- the importance of spiritual direction for a secure and more profound spiritual growth in holiness;

- to accept the divine will without annulling the human will, but to transform and illuminate it under the action of the Holy Spirit and to respond in a free, active and responsible manner;

- to love and respect creation and nature because they are gifts from God entrusted to us;

- to witness with their lives to charity, forgiveness, simplicity, humility; and to be peacemakers, " not with weapons that kill, but with the weapon of Jesus, love";

- special attention and care for the sick: " Jesus lives and is present in a particular way in every sick person". Our Lady sheds light on the meaning of suffering, which, "if accepted and united to the suffering of Jesus, will serve to bestow infinite spiritual graces, personally, for all of the holy Church and the Kingdom of God";

- to man's ultimate goal, which is eternal life with God, the soul's salvation for all eternity".

One issue that some theologians have questioned in depth is why the blood that flowed from the Madonna was male. Fr. Livio Fanzaga, director of *Radio Maria*, stressed that "we must never underestimate the signs from heaven, and in this regard, the first thing to highlight is that the blood that counts in the history of redemption is not that of Our Lady, but that of Christ. But, going further, we must not overlook the fact that the blood of Our

Lady and the blood of Jesus are the same since Jesus did not have a human father. Everything that Jesus took, as far as his humanity is concerned, he received from Mary: and therefore, in that masculinity of the blood poured out by the statue, I see the profound meaning that the humanity of Christ comes entirely from Our Lady".

In Fr. Fanzaga's opinion, "concerning what happened to Jesus in Gethsemane, an exact biblical interpretation can be proposed: "When he entered into the struggle, he prayed more intensely, and his sweat became like drops of blood falling to the ground" (*Luke* 22:44). The mystics agree that what Jesus suffered during his passion, even more than physical suffering was moral suffering, that is, the knowledge that many people would be saved by his passion, but many others would reject his gesture. In short, Jesus was oppressed by human sin, by the refusal of redemption. Our Lady's tears of blood express this same psychological pressure. Contemplating the rejected redemption, seeing "those who do not drink the blood of Christ", as St

Catherine of Siena put it, Mary feels oppression weighing on her heart that leads to this terrible weeping".

Fr. Stefano De Fiores, who taught at the prestigious Pontifical Gregorian University in Rome and was one of the world's most qualified scholars of Marian themes, agreed: "The sign of the crying of male blood recalls Christ's passion, the abyss of physical, moral and spiritual pain he suffered and offered to the Father for the salvation of humanity. In Mary's weeping, we hear the unspeakable groans of the Spirit, which are at one with the groans of creation until divine sonship is manifested in it".

In any case, Fr. De Fiores stressed, "one must discard the idea that these are metaphorical tears, that is, a pure exterior symbol without any reference to the situation of the person to whom the tears are attributed: this would be a clear case of deception or exteriority. Nor can tears of suffering, such as those she shed during her earthly life, be attributed to Mary: they would be incompatible with the state of happiness proper to eternal life. The explanation that speaks of mystical tears, as the actual repercussion of the sufferings of the Church on the Mother of the Faithful, is generally considered plausible".

Fr. Stefano De Fiores, in a particular study on the tenth anniversary of the tears, went deep into the theological meaning of the tears of blood, identifying four meanings, "starting with the Mariological one: Mary weeps for the sins and evils of the world, especially for the shedding of innocent blood, and invites to conversion. The first interpretation reads the Civitavecchia event in continuity with previous Marian manifestations, in which the Virgin revealed great concern for the world's fate. At La Salette in 1846, Our Lady appeared in tears and revealed her message without ceasing to weep. At Lourdes in 1858, the Immaculate shows a sad face when she asks Bernadette to kiss the earth in penance for sinners. Also, in Fatima in 1917, Our Lady took on a gloomy appearance, especially in the last apparition. At Syracuse in 1953, she does nothing but weeps human tears. At Civitavecchia, the Madonna sheds tears of blood.

It is a mute, silent, but tragic summary of the messages already delivered by the Mother of Jesus to the humble visionaries chosen by her. After the admonishing words, the weeping of normal tears, now even the weeping of blood... What more can Mary add to shake sleepy consciences? ".

"The second meaning is Christological: Mary weeps for the same reason that led Christ to weep and sweat blood. Jesus shed tears not only before the tomb of his friend Lazarus and during his passion but also at the sight of Jerusalem, thinking of its destruction. This is a double sin of omission: the city did not understand the way of peace, that is, of full and total salvation, and it did not recognise the time of his visit, as it did not grasp the decisive moment of the salvation offered by Jesus. Faced with this rejection, Jesus reacts with a cry of impotence and with the announcement of the terrible fate of Jerusalem. Mary cries, as did Jesus, to give society a final warning not to reject the kingdom of God and not to stubbornly reject the Gospel message. Hers is an earnest cry, full of sad omens, a reminder not to reject the divine invitations lest we incur ruin".

The Mariologist continues: "Then there is the Trinitarian interpretation: Mary weeps to manifest her mysterious suffering and the ineffable suffering of God the Father, Son and Holy Spirit. Since Mary intervenes in human history by God's mandate, Marian's manifestations are part of the divine plan of salvation and ultimately reflect the will and the face of the Trinity. Mary's tears point to God Himself and the problem of His impassibility. Today's theology shuns an apathetic image of God, which makes Him an impassive being in the face of world events. In this perspective, Mary's suffering and tears reveal the pathos of the Father, whose compassionate heart the suffering of Christ and the Church mysteriously docks".

Finally, "in reflecting on the weeping of Jesus and Mary, we must not forget the anthropological aspect, the significance of tears as a human expression with universal dimensions. Weeping is a symbol dense with meaning.

The following moving definition can be given of the tear: "A drop that is extinguished by evaporation, after having borne witness: a symbol of pain and intercession". It is a physiological form of expression provoked by a strong emotion in the face of a world of irreparably threatened values.

In the light of biblical revelation, the fundamental Christian values are communion with God, the Trinity, the purpose of the Church, fraternity, freedom, family, life... Today, these values are besieged or undermined to the extent that they jeopardise its future. It is no wonder that Mary's tears represent the denunciation of an unbearable situation for a Mother's heart, a cry of alarm that calls for the taking on of one's responsibilities to defeat an otherwise ruinous and inescapable destiny. They are a prophecy aimed at changing the world and overturning unjust situations of oppression and incoherence contrary to the plan for humanity by the God of communion and fraternity. They also hope that the sad situation full of negativity will evolve by the expectations of her maternal Heart and the desires of Christ her Son".

Caniato stated that in 2005 Jessica 'received a special visit from Our Lady, during which a detailed prayer of consecration to her Immaculate Heart was dictated to her for distribution, to which Bishop Grillo granted the imprimatur: 'Holy Virgin, moved by your maternal love, you presented yourself shedding tears of blood to remind us of the blood that Jesus shed on the cross for us sinners and to invite us to conversion. In thanksgiving and response to your maternal concern, we consecrate ourselves to your Immaculate Heart. We resolve to live our baptismal consecration, always to be united with the ecclesiastical hierarchy, to nourish ourselves with Jesus in the Eucharist, to go to confession often, to adore Jesus in the Eucharist present in the tabernacle, to pray the Holy Rosary in private or in the family and to offer up every action of the day. Holy Virgin, you have manifested yourself as Our Lady of the Roses, Queen of Families, Queen of Peace, Mother of the Church, and Queen of Heaven.

With these titles, we turn to you, trusting that you will grant us our desires. Our Lady of the Roses, obtain the graces we need and assist us in our hour of trial. Queen of Families, bless our family and grant that each family may live in peace, love, union, respect for the sacrament of marriage and Christian education for their children.

Queen of Peace, grant peace to the world: may all wars cease and brotherhood and love reign among men. Mother of the Church, defend the Church of your Son from the attacks of the Evil One and every form of division, and may every Christian live the commitments of baptism. Protect the Holy Father and all the bishops. Guide priests and consecrated souls to remain faithful to their mission and priestly/religious consecration. Queen of Heaven, grant that we may always love you as our Mother and Mother of Jesus, and after this earthly pilgrimage, welcome us next to you in the glory of Paradise to contemplate God's face and sing eternally of His mercy".

The theme of consecration is, in fact, closely linked to the event in Civitavecchia, as Fr. Pablo Martin pointed out in the letter delivered on February 4th to Bishop Grillo: "On the first Sunday of Advent, November 27th 1994, the feast of the Miraculous Medal, we made a solemn consecration of the families and the parish to Mary. After the renewal of baptismal promises, I blessed and handed the Miraculous Medal to all those present at the moment of communion. We read together a specific prayer of consecration to Our Lady, which we all signed. More than a hundred signatures expressing this solemn commitment to life have been placed together with Jesus in our tabernacle ever since. The extraordinary events that took place just over two months later convince me that the Lord has taken us seriously".

Subsequently, Monsignor Grillo had a somewhat ambiguous attitude in this regard since Our Lady had explicitly asked for the consecration. While reconstructing the story in his book, the Bishop attributed to Jessica the statement that "Our Lady would have wanted from me an *Act of Entrustment of my priests and the priests of the whole Church to the Immaculate Heart of Mary.* The little girl also recalls that Our Lady added that I should also speak to the Pope because Our Lady would have wanted the act of entrustment for the priests of the whole Church".

Fr. Flavio Ubodi commented, "it is strange how one is almost afraid to pronounce the word 'consecration' in the name of a controversial theological discourse.

If you believe the messages, you must keep to what Our Lady says through the visionaries. In a message of January 4th 1996, addressed to the bishop, we read: "Accept me officially on February 2nd... Have all the parishes and families consecrated". In the following message of February 5th of the same year, Our Lady manifested her suffering and reproach for not being listened to".

Fr. Ubodi also clarifies that the problem posed by those who affirm that consecration can only be made to God, while to Our Lady one can only make an act of entrustment to her maternal care, is false: "Firstly, because Our Lady spoke of "consecration" and not of "entrustment" to her Immaculate Heart. If Our Lady said this, there must be a reason. Consecration is a deeper act than simply entrusting; it involves and commits more; it takes one out of the profane and puts one on God's side. Secondly, it is true that consecration is made to God and takes place through Jesus Christ, the only Mediator between God and us. But the consecration also takes place through Mary, because Christ has associated her with Himself in the work of mediation and redemption".

Therefore, "consecrating oneself to the Immaculate Heart of Mary means consecrating oneself to God through the virginal hands of Mary, contemplated in her various aspects of motherhood, love and mercy. Consecrating oneself to the Immaculate Heart of Mary means giving space to the Blessed Virgin so that she may exercise her spiritual motherhood in us for our holiness and salvation. Under the pretence of "correcting" Our Lady, by replacing the term "consecration" with "entrustment", bringing in theological reasons, one could read a subtle diabolical insinuation tending to consecrate to the Lord less effective".

In this dimension, it is significant that, among the titles with which the Madonnina presented herself, there is the attribute "of the Roses". Fabio Gregori detailed that "she explained that the rose is a sign with a triple Christological connotation. First of all, its petals, which open and close around the nucleus, represent the Christian community that is in communion with Jesus, and then opens itself to the apostolate; the red colour, the most celebrated of this beloved flower, recalls the bloodshed by the Son of God during the Passion; while the perfume, the same one that many pilgrims are sure to savour in Pantano, is the same perfume of Christ. By calling herself "Our Lady of the Roses", the Virgin would thus express an intimate bond with the mission and sacrifice of her Son and, through him, with the Church of humanity".

As Father Pablo Martin pointed out on the occasion of the tenth anniversary, "the sign was given to us. After her image was brought to the church of Sant Agostino's and exposed to the veneration of the faithful, she continued to work in many hearts silently: As witnessed by the priests who hear confessions there. But since then, the sign of her tears, that little bit of blood that the tests had spared, has gradually disappeared with time and perhaps the combination of the temperature, humidity and saltiness. It is good that the photographs bear witness, although unfortunately not of all fourteen tears. Is it not to make us realise that now the signs of Mary, instead of her tears, must be us?".

TABLE OF CONTENTS

HISTORY..3

PROPHECY AND SCIENCE................…..………...37

THE MESSAGE………...…………………………….67

Made in United States
North Haven, CT
08 October 2024